To Maralyn—S.McB.

For my mother—K.L.

I'LL ALWAYS BE YOUR FRIEND

SAM McBRATNEY

ILLUSTRATIONS BY KIM LEWIS

HARPERCOLLINSPUBLISHERS

Once upon a time
there was a little fox.

The little fox and his mother were playing
in the fields. They played running games,
sneak-up-and-pounce games,

and stand-completely-still games. And when
their shadows grew long in the evening,
they played jump-over-my-shadow games.

Mother Fox looked away to where
the sun was going down.
"It's getting late," she said. "We'll stop
playing now and get ready for the night."

The little fox scampered
away through the long grass. "I'm
not coming!" he shouted. "You have to
try and find me."
Mother Fox looked over her shoulder. "It
will soon be dark," she said. "We can play
again tomorrow."

But the little fox didn't want to wait until tomorrow. He wanted to play another game and he wanted to play it now.

"I'm not your friend anymore," he said. "And I'm not going to be your friend again . . . ever."

"Oh dear, you'll never be my friend again?" asked his mother.

"No. Never ever."

The little fox lay very still in the long
grass. Everything was quiet. He watched
some tall meadow flowers swaying in the breeze.
Something fluttered above his head and, looking
up, he saw the early evening stars.
Could something be watching him?

"Well, I won't be your friend for a long time," he said.
"A long, long time."

"And how long is a long time?" called his mother.

"Until I'm big."

"Then I shall just have
to wait until you're big,"
sighed his mother.

The little fox glanced over his shoulder. Did he hear whispering behind him, or only the *swish* of the wind blowing through the meadow grass?

Something could be getting ready to chase me, he thought. Something really, really nasty with pointy teeth and sharp claws, and his mother wouldn't even know.

"Well . . . I think I might be your
friend tomorrow," he said quietly.

No answer came.

Was his mother still there?

Or was he all alone?

The little fox stood up on his back legs and saw that it *was* getting dark. There were shadows and strange shapes everywhere.

He began to run. He ran and ran from all
the things that might be just behind him!
Then. . . .

Then he saw his mother, waiting
for him in the last of the daylight.

With a rush and a hop the little fox jumped
up and held tight to his mother's soft fur, and
he knew that nothing could get to him now!

"I'm glad you might be my friend tomorrow," said his mother.

The little fox stretched up to whisper into his mother's ear. There was one more thing that he wanted to say.

"You don't have to wait until tomorrow, I am your friend now."

"Oh, good." His mother smiled as the little fox settled down to sleep.

"That's very good," she said softly in the dark, "because I'm your friend, too. And do you know what? I'll always be your friend."